Laugh Lines

written
by
Carol Costa

Ten royalty free skits serve as examples for lessons
on comedy writing and performing.

TABLE OF CONTENTS

INTRODUCTION

Introduction

I began my writing career as a journalist and short story author. After some limited success, a friend came to me with an idea he had for a comedy skit about vampires. He had come up with humorous names for the characters and a partial storyline, but didn't know how to put a script together. I used the characters and expanded the storyline, putting my own spin on it.

Our church used the skit called, "The Night Life of a Vampire," in a fundraising variety show. I worked backstage for the show. I waited in the wings for the first laugh line hoping the audience would react to it. The actor said the line and the audience roared with laughter. I was delighted and was totally hooked on live theater and comedy writing from then on.

A short time later, another writer and I were asked to create skits for a variety show. The theme of this show was the 1940's. We went to the university library and got audio tapes of old radio shows. I grew up listening to some of these shows, but now, I concentrated on the laugh lines and the gimmicks that reached across time to make people laugh. Two of the skits in this book are ones written for that show based on what we learned from the great comedy that did not need visual effects to enhance them. Of course, in live stage and television visual comedic elements are standard.

Before each comedy skit in this book you will find information on how the idea was conceived and the comedic elements were set up and the laugh lines delivered.

Since every skit has been performed in theaters and on radio programs, there will also be tips and suggestions you can review before including them in classes or production.

THE DOCTORS ARE SMOOTH OPERATORS

Having grown up watching television soap operas, I was very familiar with their standard storylines. All the characters had secrets. Affairs, addictions, illegitimate children, and lost love were most common. When I watched medical soap operas with doctors had many personal problems, I would think "I would hate to be a patient these doctors were treating."

When I was asked to write a comedy skit about soap operas, I decided to take use of the old standard theme and give it a new twist. Instead of hiding their secrets, as they commonly do in the TV shows, the characters in this skit would tell all.

As the scene opens, an unsuspecting patient awaits surgery in one of these television hospitals. The two doctors and a nurse begin confessing, complaining, and arguing about their secrets and problems.

All comedy lines require set up and delivery. In this skit, most of the set ups are voiced by the doctors. The Nurse must take it all seriously as they reveal their secrets to the patient who becomes more and more upset by their revelations.

The Doctors Are Smooth Operators

Cast of Characters

The Patient: (any age, male or female)

The Nurse: (any age, female)

Dr. Brown: (male) an older surgeon

Dr. Jay: (male) younger doctor

Amelia: (female) Dr. Jay's crazy wife

Set and Props: A table or hospital gurney for the doctors and nurse to surround. Hospital gown for the patient. Scrubs and surgical equipment for doctors and nurse. Baby doll for Amelia.

At Rise: DOCTOR BROWN, DOCTOR JAY, and NURSE surround PATIENT.

DR. BROWN: (*To Dr. Jay*) Are you ready for surgery, my boy? (*He turns to the patient*) I call him my boy because I just found out that he is the product of a love affair I once had with my best friend's wife.

NURSE: The poor woman died, but not before she wrote a letter requesting that Dr. Brown, here, be told the truth only if their son's life was in danger.

DR. BROWN: Which it was after he tried to commit suicide.

DR. JAY: I was depressed about all those patients who died on the operating table.

(Patient sits up and tries to get off the table.)

PATIENT: You know, I'm suddenly feeling much better.

(Dr. Jay pushes the patient back down on the table.)

DR. JAY: Relax. That all happened weeks ago when I was hooked on drugs. I'm fine now.

NURSE: (*Soothingly to patient*) Yes, don't worry. You're in excellent hands. These doctors have performed this operation
lots of times, when they've been more upset than they are today.

PATIENT: Oh no. Why are they upset?

NURSE: I probably shouldn't tell you this, but this morning, Dr. Jay's wife, Amelia, escaped from the mental institution.

DR. BROWN: Poor Amelia, one minute she was performing surgery and the next, she snapped. (*He snaps his fingers.*)

PATIENT: She was a doctor?

DR. JAY: Yes, we met at medical school.

(Overcome with grief, DR. JAY covers his face with his hands.)

PATIENT: Oh, you poor man.

NURSE: Don't waste your sympathy on him. Since Amelia's been locked up, he's completed more passes than the Arizona Cardinals.

DR. JAY: Don't listen to her. She's jealous. She's always wanted me for herself.

DR. BROWN: That's not true. She's in love with me.

PATIENT: This is terrible!

DR. BROWN: I'll tell you what's terrible. I faint at the sight of blood

PATIENT: But how can you be a surgeon?

NURSE: Oh, don't worry. After you're asleep, we'll blindfold him.

PATIENT: (*Screaming.*) Let me out of here.

(*Patient tries to get off the cart again, but Dr. Jay pushes her down again.*)

DR. JAY: Oh, lay down and stop complaining. We've got an important issue to discuss here.

PATIENT: About my surgery?

DR. JAY: No, about who this nurse is really in love with. Okay, Florence Nightingale, make your choice, me or my dad?

NURSE: I think you're both losers. Besides, my heart belongs to George.

PATIENT: Who is George?

DR. BROWN: George was her first three husbands. The first time George left her for another woman. The second time he ran away to join the circus, and the third time...

NURSE: He didn't mean to leave me the last time. His plane crashed in the ocean.

DR. JAY: They never found his body, so she's waiting for him to surface again.

NURSE: George is an excellent swimmer.

PATIENT: Right. Can you put me to sleep now?

(*Amelia rushes in carrying a doll.*)

DR. JAY: Oh no. It's my crazy wife, Amelia

AMELIA: Don't get excited, lover boy. I just came by to drop off the baby. You and Grandpa, here, can baby sit.

PATIENT: Baby? Lady, that's not a baby. It's only a...

(*Nurse places her hand over patient's mouth stopping her/him from completing the sentence as Amelia croons and rocks the doll.*)

NURSE: Shh! You mustn't tell her that. She thinks that doll is the child she could never have.

PATIENT: Is that what drove her crazy?

NURSE: I think so. Although some people think it was the sex change operation. Here, hold this will you?

(*Nurse hands patient her clipboard. Then the Nurse, and the Doctors gather around Amelia, ignoring the patient. The patient writes something on the clipboard and then gets off the cart and runs off.*)

DR. BROWN: Now, Amelia, you know we only want what's best for you, so you're going to have to go back to the mental institution where you belong.

AMELIA: I'm not going back there. Here, take the kid. I'm going to meet George.

DR. JAY: George is dead.

AMELIA: So, that's why he hasn't called me lately. Oh well, it's okay. I'm sure I'll find someone else.

(*They begin thrusting the doll back and forth at each other.*)

DR. BROWN: Please, Amelia, be reasonable. We can't baby sit right now. Can't you see we're about to operate on this patient?

(*Amelia looks past him at the empty table.*)

AMELIA: What patient?

(*The other three turn to see that she is right. The patient is gone.*)

DR. BROWN: Oops. We've lost another one.

(*The Nurse picks up the clipboard left on the table.*)

NURSE: At least this one left a note.

(*Dr. Jay grabs the clipboard and reads the note aloud.*)

DR. JAY: I've gone to take Amelia's place at the mental institution. Anyone who comes to this hospital for surgery, definitely needs their head examined.

The End

THE EX-TERMINATOR

This skit was originally written to be used in front of the curtain to allow the stage crew to change out the set during a variety show.

This skit uses two standard comedy elements: Misunderstanding and surprise. These two elements put the characters into an awkward situation. This allows the characters to begin alternating between set up and delivery of the laugh lines.

Performing notes:

Both actors should be motivated by their desire to survive an embarrassing situation.

The Ex Terminator

Cast of Characters

Interviewer: (any age, male or female)

Arnold: (male) Exterminator

Set: Can be done on an empty stage or in front of a curtain

Props and Costumes: Work clothes for Arnold and an exterminating pack with nozzle and hose. A paper with a list of questions for Interviewer.

At Rise: INTERVIEWER enters and speaks to audience.

INTERVIEWER: When the director of this show asked me if I could find a special guest to make an appearance, I never thought I would be standing here introducing a person who is known all over the world for his films. Best of all, he agreed to come here with the costume and props that have made him a star. To be honest, I was shocked when he called me and asked me to book him for this appearance. (*Holds up a list.*) I have a list of good questions I am going to ask him. So, hold onto your seats, folks, and welcome, Arnold The Terminator.

(*Arnold enters in his work clothes carrying his exterminating equipment. He smiles and waves at the audience. Interviewer is shocked.*)

ARNOLD: Thank you. It's a pleasure to be here.

INTERVIEWER: Oh no. You're not the right Arnold. I'll bet you're not even in show business.

ARNOLD: I am in the bug business.

INTERVIEWER: When you called, I asked if you were Arnold, the Terminator, and you said you were the Ex-Terminator. I thought you were being funny because you moved on to other acting roles. And when I asked you why you didn't have an accent, you said you dropped it, so you could run for president.

ARNOLD: That was just my little joke. So, can we get on with the interview now? I've been practicing those lines you told me to say.

INTERVIEWER: What lines?

ARNOLD: (*Striking a pose.*) Hasta La Vista, baby. It's not a tumor.

INTERVIEWER: Very good. You can leave now.

ARNOLD: I got all dressed up to come over here. I even gave up my gig to call Bingo at the Elks Lodge because you promised to interview me.

INTERVIEWER: But you are not the man I thought you were.

ARNOLD: My wife says that to me all the time.... but she is stuck with me...and so are you.

INTERVIEWER: But the questions I have are for the other Arnold.

ARNOLD: I am not leaving this stage until you interview me like you promised. Just read the first question on that list you have.

INTERVIEWER: Okay. First question, how did you get all those muscles?

ARNOLD: No mussels. I'm allergic to sea food. Next question?

(*Interviewer looks at the list and then throws it away.*)

INTERVIEWER: Oh, brother. Let's just find out more about you, Arnold. You said you have a wife. Tell us about her.

ARNOLD: My wife is not an easy woman to live with. Just last night we had a big fight about her political ambitions.

INTERVIEWER: How did the fight end?

ARNOLD: My wife got down on her knees.

INTERVIEWER: She was apologizing to you?

ARNOLD: No. She was trying to coax me out from under the bed. She's one tough mama.

INTERVIEWER: You said your wife has political ambitions?

ARNOLD: Yes. She thinks she will be living in the White House someday.

INTERVIEWER: And how do you feel about that?

ARNOLD: The White House would be the perfect place for me.

INTERVIEWER: Why is that?

ARNOLD: Who else could get all the bugs out of the oval office.

(Arnold holds up exterminating gear. Interviewer groans and runs off stage.)

ARNOLD: *(Speaking to the audience.)* This interview may be over, but I'll be back!
The End

MAGIC

The idea for this skit was inspired by a friend who was taking lessons on magic tricks. It turned out that he was not very good, but his struggles were amusing. This coupled with magicians that used audience members in their shows gave me another way to complicate an inept magician's act.

A basic tool in comedy writing is to take a common element and make it unusual. Most people chosen to take part in a magician's act are very cooperative, but what if they were difficult and refused to follow instructions. Thinking about basic concepts of a subject and asking yourself "What if?" often results in a comic situation.

Since we are talking about changing things this skit is a good one for aspiring writers to use for practice. Take this skit and rewrite it. For example, make it a high school talent show and change the ages of the characters to teenagers. This of course means you will have to adjust the actions and dialogue of the characters. The most important thing for a writer is to get started. The act of putting your ideas in a written format opens up your mind and imagination to your own magic.

Performing this skit only requires that you have fun with it regardless of the ages of the characters you are portraying.

Magic

Cast of Characters:

Announcer: (male or female)

Mr. Abracadabra: (male or female) Magician

Lizzie: Mature Woman

Sonny: (male) Large and intimidating.

SET AND PROPS: Bare Stage with small table
Mr. Abracadabra's case, containing a deck of cards, a pair of scissors, and a magic wand, tie for Sonny to wear.

At Rise: Lights up on a bare stage

ANNOUNCER O.S.: And now ladies and gentleman, straight from a one night stand at George's hardware store in Kokomo,Indiana, We are proud to present a young man who will baffle you…with his magic that is…Mr. Abracadabra!

(*MR. ABRACADABRA enters, carrying his case and tripping a little. He sets his case on the table and opens it and takes out a deck of cards.*)

MR. ABRACADABRA: Thank you and good evening, ladies and gentlemen. For the first trick of the evening, we have chosen a volunteer from the audience. May I have the volunteer, please.

(Lizzie enters and waves at the audience:

LIZZIE: Hi everyone. My name is Elizabeth, but you all can call me, Lizzie.

MR. ABRACADABRA: Welcome, Lizzie. Now, please tell the audience...Have I ever seen you before?

LIZZIE: Of course you have, back stage. Don't you remember?

MR. ABRACADABRA: Sure, lady, but I meant I've never seen you before tonight. Isn't that right?

LIZZIE: Yes.

MR. ABRACADABRA: Good.

LIZZIE: Good? That's an awful thing to say to a person, like you're glad you've never seen me before.

MR. ABRACADABRA: (*Getting nervous.*) Now, madam, don't be ridiculous.

LIZZIE: (*Yelling.*) Ridiculous! Oh, swell, now you're calling me names. I mean, I'm nice enough to come up here and be a volunteer, and you call me names.

MR. ABRACADABRA: Look, I swear, I think you're a perfectly lovely person, and I'm very sorry that I haven't had the previous pleasure of knowing you….Okay?..Now, let's get on with the trick, shall we?

LIZZIE: Okay, smart guy. What's the trick?

(*MR. ABRACADABRA holds out a deck of cards and fans them in front of her.*)

MR. ABRACADABRA: Take a card, any card, and don't let me see it.

(*Lizzie takes a card, looks at it and puts it behind her back.*)

MR. ABRACADABRA: Good! Now, did you look at the card carefully, so you'll remember it?

LIZZIE: I got it.

MR. ABRACADABRA: Fine, then place put the card back into the deck.

LIZZIE: Why?

MR. ABRACADABRA: Because that's the way the trick is done.

LIZZIE: Oh no, you don't. I'm not falling for that old line.

MR. ABRACADABRA: (*Getting upset.*) What old line?

LIZZIE: I know what you're up to. You get me to put the card back, and then you'll pull out another one, and I won't remember if it's the right card or not.

MR. ABRACADABRA: (*With forced patience.*) But I thought you just told me that you had the card memorized.

LIZZIE: I did, but my memory ain't what it used to be, so I'll just keep the card, thank you.

MR. ABRACADABRA: (*Firmly.*) Put the card back in the deck, so we can get on with the trick.

LIZZIE: I'm not going to do it. If you're really a magician, you'll be able to tell what it is while I keep it right here in my hand.

MR. ABRACADABRA: (*Yelling at her.*) Of course, I'm really a magician, but I can't do that.

LIZZIE: You're gonna have to,'cause I'm not giving this card back until you do.

MR. ABRACADABRA: (*Frustrated.*) All right! The Ace of Hearts!

LIZZIE: (*Smugly*) Wrong!

MR. ABRACADABRA: The Two of Diamonds?

LIZZIE: Nope.

MR. ABRACADABRA: (*Yelling again.*) The Three of Spades!

LIZZIE: Wrong again. Guess you're not such a smart guy now, are you?

MR. ABRACADABRA: Give me that card.

LIZZIE: No.

MR. A: Give me that card, you old bat!

(MR. ABRACADABRA *tries to grab her, but she screams and runs off stage. Suddenly, the magician remembers he is in front of an audience. He turns and smiles.*)

MR. ABRACADABRA: Wasn't she great, folks? Let's have a big hand for the little lady. It was all part of the act, you know.

(*MR. ABRACADABRA claps and the audience may or may not join him.*)

MR. ABRACADABRA: Can I have the next volunteer, please?

(*Sonny enters wearing a necktie.*)

MR. ABRACADABRA: Good evening, sir. Have I ever seen you before?

SONNY: Sure, you have…

MR. ABRACADABRA: Of course, backstage…I know… Let's get on with the trick. That's a beautiful tie you're wearing.

SONNY: Thank you. It's my favorite.

(*MR. ABRACADABRA takes out a pair of scissors, grabs the tie and cuts it in half.*)

SONNY: (*Yelling.*) Hey! What's the big idea?

(*Sonny grabs hold of the magician and prepares to punch him.*)

MR. ABRACADABRA: (*Very nervously.*) Please, sir, it's part of the trick. I'll fix it.

SONNY: How are you gonna fix it?

MR. ABRACADABRA: By magic, of course. But first you have to let me go.

(*Sonny reluctantly lets him go.*)

MR. ABRACADABRA: Now, in order for this trick to work, you must close your eyes good and tight and not open them until I tell you.

SONNY: Okay. I will shut my eyes, but this better work.

MR. ABRACADABRA: Trust me.

(*Holding the two pieces of the tie together Mr. A takes out his magic wand waves it over the tie. It doesn't work. He tries again. It still doesn't work.*)

SONNY: Is it fixed yet?

MR. ABRACADABRA: Just be patient, sir. Some spells take a little longer than others.

SONNY: (*Angrily.*) My mother gave me that tie, and if you don't fix it, I'm going to beat the daylights out of you.

(*MR. ABRACADABRA waves his want again, but the tie is still in two pieces. He stands and faces the audience.*)

MR. ABRACADABRA: Ladies and gentleman, for my final trick of the evening.....Mr. Abracadabra will disappear!

(*MR. ABRACADABRA runs off the stage, leaving his case and magic wand behind. Sonny opens his eyes and sees that his tie is ruined.*)

SONNY: (*Stomping his feet.*) My tie! My favorite tie!

(LIZZIE returns.)

LIZZIE: Shut up, Sonny, I'll fix your tie.

SONNY: How are you gonna' do that?

(*LIZZIE picks up MR. ABRACADABRA'S magic wand*)

LIZZIE: By magic, of course....

The End

MYSTERY THEATER

The idea for this skit came from a comedy segment I saw on television. I took the idea of a radio show with an inept sound effects person and created my own original story around that idea.

So, let me explain why using someone's idea is perfectly all right. An idea cannot be copyrighted. Writing teachers often give a single idea to a class and tell them to write a story based on that idea. Each student will write a different story on that same idea. The idea cannot be copyrighted, but each student's original story can be copyrighted.

I once took a class on screenwriting and one person in the class was really worried about people stealing her idea. Here is what the instructor told us. "The only time you should worry about your idea being stolen, is if you think it is the last good idea you will ever have."

As you will see in this skit, the sound effects person is only funny because he/she disrupts the main story in the skit which is the mystery that has to be solved. Any writer can take the idea of an out of control sound effects person and create a primary story to for it.

Performing this skit requires that the radio stars to display a range of emotions. While the crazy sound effects upset them, they must not show the amusement the audience is projecting. These two must overcome their annoyance and save the show. The sound effects actor has to concentrate on producing the wrong sound effects at the right times for this skit to work.

Mystery Theater

Cast of Characters:

Announcer: (male or female)

Betty: Actress

Jason: Actor

Sound Effects (SFX) Person

SET: Old time radio studio, where a show is about to go on the air.

Furniture and Props: Standing Microphone for actors, Chair behind the table with sound effects, thunder, telephone ring, school bell, whistle, gun with blanks for gun shots, whiskey bottle

AT RISE: *BETTY & JASON are standing in place, silently looking at their scripts.*

(*SFX Person enters singing loudly and holding a whiskey bottle, and falls into the chair and smiles and waves at the actors.*)

BETTY: Oh no! He/she is drunk again. We can't go on the air with him/her like that.

JASON: We'll have to. It's almost air time. It'll be okay. I've seen him/her in worst shape.

BETTY: I hope you're right.

ANNOUNCER O.S: Good evening and welcome to Mystery Theater. Tonight's episode is MIDNIGHT TRAIN TO GEORGIA.

SFX: TRAIN WHISTLE (*Since sound man does that fine, Jason & Betty relax a bit.*)

ANNOUNCER: As our story opens, Inspector Jason is questioning Mrs. Horace Willoughby on the death of her husband.

JASON: I'm sorry to trouble you at a time like this, but I must ask you a few questions.

BETTY: I'll try to help you...(*She sobs.*) Oh, what will I do without my poor Horace.(*She sobs.*)

SFX: HORSE NEIGH (*Betty & Jason are shocked but continue to read their lines. The Sound person is weaving around barely able to stay on his chair.*)

JASON: Please try to control yourself, Mrs. Willoughby.

BETTY: It's this awful storm. Thunder always makes me so nervous.

(*The actors wait for the SFX of thunder that doesn't come, because the SFX person is trying to get a drink from his/her bottle.*)

BETTY: I said...thunder always makes me so nervous.

(*No thunder, so the actors continue*)

JASON: Can you tell me what time your husband was murdered?

BETTY: I found his body around midnight. I remember because the train whistle was blowing.

JASON: Ah, yes, the train to Georgia. The whistle blows at six and at midnight. People in this town set their clocks by it. It's six o'clock now. Let's listen for the train.

SFX: THUNDER   (*Betty & Jason react to the mistake, but they are helpless, and try to cover for the drunken sound man.*)

BETTY: Too bad we couldn't hear it with all the thunder. Anyway, I found poor Horace...

SX: HORSE NEIGH

BETTY: (*continuing to speak.*) on the kitchen floor with a knife in his back. I'd just come home from the late show at the Palace, where I'd been all night.

JASON: Who else was in the house?

SFX: TELEPHONE RINGING (*Since the script doesn't call for a phone ringing at this time, the actors look at each other in panic and again try to cover.*)

BETTY: Were you expecting a call, Inspector?

JASON: Not yet. I have more questions to ask.

SFX: THE TELEPHONE CONTINUES TO RING

(*Sound person has fallen asleep leaning on the telephone.*)

BETTY: I guess one of us had better answer it.

(*Betty hurries over to wake up the sound person, while Jason pretends to answer the phone.*)

JASON: Hello.

RINGING CONTINUES

(*Betty shakes him/her and the drunk falls off the chair and the SFX stops. Betty is getting the drunk back in the chair while Jason ad libs.*)

JASON: I'm sorry, you have the wrong number.

(*BETTY returns to her place.*)

BETTY: You were saying, Inspector?

Jason: Now, Mrs. Willoughby, I was asking who else was in the house when you discovered your husband's body?

(*SFX person is looking at his script, trying to find his place. Gives up and throws it on the floor as BETTY says her line.*)

SFX: THUNDER

(*Realizing her line could not be heard, BETTY yells it just as SFX stops.*)

BETTY: (*Yelling loudly.*)No one except the butler, of course.

(*JASON now tries to cover for BETTY.*)

JASON: There's no need to shout, Mrs. Willoughby.

BETTY: You're right. I'm getting hoarse.

SFX: HORSE NEIGH

BETTY: No...no...I meant my voice was a little hoarse.

SFX: SMALLER HORSE NEIGH.

JASON: All right...let me see if I have all of this. It was midnight...Your husband was stabbed in the kitchen and only you and the butler were in the house.

BETTY: You'd better hurry and solve this case, Inspector. We're running out of time.

JASON: I'll have the solution momentarily. As soon as my assistant calls.

(*SFX person is sleeping again.*)

JASON: (*Yelling at SFX person.*) The phone call should be coming in right now.

(*No response. JASON yells louder.*)
 He always RINGS me on time.

SFX: SCHOOL BELL (*A distraught JASON takes what he can get.*)

JASON: Hello....yes...yes...I have it. Thank you for calling.

BETTY: What is it Inspector?

JASON: I know who killed your husband.

BETTY: You do?

JASON: It was you, Mrs. Willoughby.

BETTY: That's ridiculous. I told you I was out until midnight.

JASON: You lied. My assistant checked your story. The midnight train didn't blow its whistle last night. The engineer said it was out of order.

BETTY: All right, Inspector. I did it! But you'll not live to tell anyone. I'm going to stab you just like I did Horace.

SFX: HORSE NEIGH.

JASON: No, put that knife away.

SFX: GUN SHOTS

JASON: You missed me! You'll never get away with this.

28

SFX: GUN SHOTS

JASON: Especially with such a noisy knife! It's over, Mrs. Willoughby. From the beginning I knew your story had a false ring.

SFX: SCHOOL BELL

BETTY: You won't take me alive. I still have the knife. I'll slash my wrists...

SFX: GUN SHOTS

JASON: You don't have the guts. Come on, we're going to the station.

SFX: TRAIN WHISTLE

JASON: (Yelling.) Not that station!!

(Betty and Jason run over to SFX person who is about to take another drink, JASON grabs the bottle the bottle as they exit and SFX person runs after them.)

The End

SECTION EIGHT

When I was asked to write a comedy skit about the army, I had no idea of what was funny about being in the army. So, I began asking people who had been in the military for help. Everyone I asked said the same thing. Nothing was funny about the army and the only thing they remembered was how much they wanted to get out of it. That led me to another comedy idea on television. The television show "Mash" had a character who was trying to get discharged by pretending to be crazy.

Again, I took an idea and created my own story around it. Again, I asked myself "What if??" I knew that a doctor had to certify that a person was insane in order for him/her to be let out of the army and I decided that the doctor in my skit would be as crazy as the people he was interviewing. This became the surprise twist at the end of my skit.

There are some funny visual elements in this skit that work well in stage productions. There are also a number of laugh lines between the doctor and his would-be patients. Costumes, props, and make up are also important to the story. Writing these things into your comedy are part of the fun.

Performing a skit like this requires that the actors exaggerate the character they are portraying and have as much fun doing it as the audience will have seeing and hearing it.

Section Eight

Cast of Characters:

Army Doctor: (male)

Nurse: (female)

First Recruit: (male)

Second Recruit- (male or female)

Third Recruit- (male or female)

SET: Army Doctor's Office with a desk, two chairs

COSTUMES AND PROPS: Women's clothes, red dots, top hat and cane, telephone

AT RISE: *DOCTOR is seated behind his desk talking on the telephone.*

DOCTOR: Yes, dear, I'll try to be home early...Don't worry, I'll call you before I leave the office, so you'll have plenty of time to get ready...

(*Nurse enters and DOCTOR hangs up the telephone.*)

NURSE: It's another group of new recruits.

DOCTOR: Oh, no, not again!

NURSE: I'm afraid so. Their Sergeants sent them over for you to evaluate.

DOCTOR: Very well, send them in...one at a time, please.

NURSE: Yes, doctor.

(*Nurse exits and a few seconds later, the FIRST RECRUIT enters dressed like a woman. The Doctor shakes his head and the man sits down in the chair next to the Doctor's desk.*)

DOCTOR: I'm going to ask you a few questions, Private.

FIRST RECRUIT: Sure. Whatever you say, doc.

DOCTOR: How do you like the army, so far?

FIRST RECRUIT: The food's great, but my mattress is a little lumpy. I got real delicate skin.

DOCTOR: I see that you prefer, shall we say, colorful clothing. Do you have any trouble finding things in your size?

FIRST RECRUIT: Hey, you know how it is, doc. They just don't make stylish shoes in a size twelve. What I wouldn't give for a pair of wedgies.

DOCTOR: I'll speak to Sergeant Monahan about that. You can wait outside.

FIRST RECRUIT: Thanks, doc. You're okay.

(*FIRST RECRUIT exits smiling, and giving the doctor a finger wave. SECOND RECRUIT enters. This one has big red spots all over her face. She sits.*)

DOCTOR: According to your file, you enlisted and then after two days had to be sent to the infirmary. Is that correct?

SECOND RECRUIT: Yes, sir.

DOCTOR: And just what do you think caused those huge red spots on your face?

(SECOND RECRUIT screams and jumps to her feet. She begins running around in circles)

SECOND RECRUIT :(Yelling) Spots? I've got spots?

DOCTOR: I'm afraid so.

SECOND RECRUIT: The army gave me spots! Wait until my mother hears about this...she'll call her congressman, she'll call the president.

(*The SECOND RECRUIT begins to sob. The NURSE enters and leads her away. They exit.*)

DOCTOR: (*Calling after them.*) Send in the next one.

(*The THIRD RECRUIT enters stands at attention and salutes the doctor.*)

DOCTOR: At ease, Private. Have a seat.

(THIRD RECRUIT *sits on the chair.*)

THIRD RECRUIT: Thank you, Mr. President. It was good of you to see me on such short notice.

DOCTOR:(*Puzzled.*)Mr. President?

(*THIRD RECRUIT reaches for the silent telephone, Picks it up and speaks into it.*)

THIRD RECRUIT: General MacArthur speaking...yes...(*Angrily.*) What? How could you let a thing like that happen? Confine yourself to quarters immediately.

(THIRD RECRUIT slams down the phone and shakes his head)

DOCTOR: Is something wrong, General?

THIRD RECRUIT: It's the Chinese, sir. They've done it again.

DOCTOR: You mean the Japanese. Have they attacked Pearl Harbor again?

THIRD RECRUIT: Pearl Harbor has nothing to do with this, sir. She can take care of her own laundry. It's mine that's ruined. Those darn Chinese put starch in everything!

DOCTOR:(*Exasperated.*) General, would you mind waiting outside? The first lady wants to speak to me.

THIRD RECRUIT: Of course, sir. We can't keep Eleanor waiting.

(*THIRD RECRUIT stands, salutes again, and marches off stage. NURSE enters.*)

NURSE: Boy, that group was the best we've had in weeks. Very ingenious. I liked the one with the spots the best.

DOCTOR: These people will try anything to make me think they're crazy, so they can get out of the army on a Section Eight. Let's give them all a clean bill of health and
recommend them for permanent KP duty.

NURSE: Yes, sir. You know, doctor, the army is very fortunate to have a man like you, who can see through all their nutty schemes. Some doctors might be fooled, by them, but not you, sir.

DOCTOR: Why, thank you, nurse.

NURSE: Well, I'll be leaving with them, doctor, so goodnight and have a nice weekend.

DOCTOR: I will. Goodnight.

(*DOCTOR waits until NURSE exits, then picks up the phone and makes a call.*)

DOCTOR: Ginger? Fred, here. I'm on my way home. Tell the orchestra to start warming up. I found a new dancing partner.

(*DOCTOR hangs up the phone, takes out his top hat and cane and begins to dance around. The* FIRST RECRUIT, *still in drag, enters and whirls around with the doctor. Then, they dance off the stage together.*)

The End

THE LISTING APPOINTMENT

This script was written for a charity show sponsored by the Tucson Board of Realtors. I worked as a real estate agent for eight years and during that time I encountered some really difficult people and situations. This script is a good example of how you can use the weird experiences in your life to enhance your comedy writing.

The humorous conflicts between the four characters change as the story moves forward. Notice how the characters take turns with the set up and delivery of the laugh lines. There is also visual comedy and action that adds to the humor.

The challenge for actors performing this script is in the changing of the attitudes between the married couple and the two agents. Maxine has one of the best laugh lines when she tells Ben that taking her along got him the listing. This line has to be delivered smugly with a triumphant smile.

The Listing Appointment

Cast of Characters:

Ben: New Real Estate Agent

Maxine: Experienced Real Estate Agent

Agnes Bagley: Homeowner wife to John Bagley

Jo. hn Bagley: Home owner husband to Agnes Bagley

SET: Living room of Bagley house. Room is made up with some furniture and some type of barricade dividing the room in half.

MAXINE O.S.: Hi Ben. Where are you going?

BEN O.S.: Great news, Maxine. A Mrs. Bagley just called and asked me to come right over. She wants to sell her house and said Magic Carpet Realty was recommended to her.

MAXINE O.S.: Good, but you're still in training. You should take a more experienced agent with you. I'm available.

BEN O.S: (*Indignant.*) I am no longer in training, and I'm quite confident I can handle a simple listing appointment on my own.

MAXINE O.S.: Suit yourself, but don't say I didn't offer to help.

BEN O.S.: I'd better go. See you later.

BEN O.S.: The house is lovely, Mrs. Bagley, just lovely. I really liked the family room. Do the draperies stay with the house?

AGNES O.S.: Yes, and I'll leave the fireplace tools also.

BEN O.S.: Very good. I'll make a note of that.

(*BEN and AGNES enter the Living Room.*)

AGNES: This is the living room. As you can see it's quite large.

BEN: Yes, it is...eh...that's a nice gun collection you have there.

AGNES: (*Indifferently.*) Oh those...They belong to Mr. Bagley.

BEN: They're very impressive...eh...Mrs. Bagley, may I ask what those barricades are doing across the center of the room?

AGNES: Oh, don't pay any attention to those. John put them up. He's always doing something stupid like that.

JOHN O.S.: (*Yelling.*) I heard that, Agnes!

AGNES: (*Yelling back.*) So you heard? Who cares?

BEN: Is that your husband?

AGNES: (*Firmly.*) Ex-husband. We're getting a divorce. That's why we're selling the house.

JOHN O.S.:(Yelling.) We're not selling!

AGNES: (*Yelling back.*) Yes, we are!

BEN: (*Slightly nervous.*) Pardon me, Mrs. Bagley, but there seems to be a difference of opinion here. I mean, you called
and said you wanted to sell your house, but it
sounds like your husband....

AGNES: (*Interrupting.*)
Ex-husband.

BEN: Ex-husband, doesn't want to sell.

AGNES: So? Who cares what he wants? I hate this house. I never wanted to buy it in the first place.

(*JOHN enters.*)

JOHN: That's not true, Agnes. Buying this house was all your idea. (*To BEN*)
You see what I've had to put up with all these years. The woman is a pain in the ...

AGNES: (*Interrupting him.*) John Bagley, don't you use profanity in front of me. I won't stand for it.

JOHN: Fine. Then why don't you sit down on what you give me a pain in.

BEN: Now, folks, please, let's not argue. Maybe we could all sit down and talk this over.

AGNES: There's nothing to discuss. Half of this house belongs to me, and I'm selling it.

JOHN: Oh yeah? Well, the other half belongs to me, and I'm not selling.

BEN: I think we may have a problem here.

JOHN: (*Yelling again.*) That's right. And her name is Agnes!

AGNES: There he goes again. You see how he blames me for everything. Just ignore him. I can't wait to sell my half of this house so I can get away from this bozo.

BEN: (*Surprised.*) You mean that you called me over here expecting me to list only half the house?

AGNES: Certainly. I only want what I'm entitled to, and that's half of everything.

BEN: But Mrs. Bagley, I can't sell half a house.

AGNES: Why not? You've seen the kitchen, family room, bedroom, patio and swimming pool. What more could anyone ask for?

JOHN: (*Laughing.*) How about a bathroom? That's over here on my side?

BEN: He's right, ma'am. That would be a big drawback.

AGNES: (Angrily.) I'm your client. Why are you taking his side?

BEN: I'm not taking anyone's side. If Mr. Bagley had been the one who called me, I would have to tell him the same thing. I can't sell half a house.

JOHN: (*Indignantly.*) And what's wrong with my side? I've got the bathroom, remember?

AGNES: (*To JOHN.*) And you need it on your side, because you're so full of...

JOHN: (*Interrupting.*) Agnes...please, you mustn't talk like that in front of a stranger.

BEN: Well, it's been lovely meeting you folks, but I must be leaving now.

(*BEN starts to leave, but Agnes grabs hold of his arm and stops him.*)

AGNES: Where are you going? You can't come in here and start all this trouble and then just walk out on us.

BEN: (*Annoyed.*) Trouble? I've done nothing. It's not my fault you two are getting a divorce.

AGNES: (*Getting angry.*) It's not my fault. I've given him the best years of my life.

JOHN: She did do that. 1998 and 99, and it's been downhill ever since.

BEN: I really think you folks should be discussing this privately.

AGNES: Why? Everyone knows what a bum he is.

JOHN: (*Angrily.*) That's not true, Agnes.

BEN: He looks like a fine fellow to me.

AGNES: Oh really? Well, you don't know how lazy he is. I can't get him to do a thing around this house.

JOHN: What do you mean? I'm always fixing things around here.

AGNES: (*Sarcastically.*) Sure, he fixes things, all right. Things like martinis, manhattans, bourbon on the rocks…

BEN: (*Yelling.*) Now stop it! I'm a real estate agent, not a marriage counselor. And really, Mrs. Bagley, I think it was awful of you to have me come over here when you knew that your husband didn't want to sell. My time is valuable, and I can't afford to waste it on nuts like you.

AGNES: (*Indignant.*) Well, that's a fine way to speak to a client.

JOHN: I'll handle this, Agnes.

(*JOHN pulls out one of his guns and points it at Ben.*)

BEN: Hey, don't point that gun at me. It makes me very nervous.

AGNES: Shoot him, John.

BEN: (*Upset.*) Are you crazy, lady? Why should he shoot me? I didn't do anything wrong?

JOHN: Oh, no? How about coming over here and trying to persuade my wife to sell this house right out from under me?

AGNES: Yes. How could you do such a thing? Don't you have any ethics?

BEN: (*Exasperated.*) Mrs. Bagley, you're the one who called me.

AGNES: (*Stubbornly.*) Well, you shouldn't have come.

BEN: You're right about that.

AGNES: (*Crying again.*) You've really upset me now. I love this house and selling it is very traumatic.

BEN: A few minutes ago, you said you hated this house and couldn't wait to sell it and get away from this bozo.

AGNES: (*Yelling.*) Don't you call my husband a bozo!

BEN: (*Yelling back.*) Well, he is a bozo. And so are you!

JOHN: That's it. I'm going to shoot him, Agnes.

AGNES: Go ahead. He deserves it.

BEN: (*Angrily.*) Oh, knock it off with those stupid threats. I know you're just bluffing.

(SFX)(GUN SHOTS)

BEN: So you're not bluffing, but I'm not going to make it easy on you.

(*BEN ducks and weaves as John keeps firing at him. BEN picks up loose objects and throws them at him. Then, then runs out of the house.*)

AGNES: You missed him again, John! He got away.

JOHN: (*Laughing.*) He made a clean getaway, Agnes.

AGNES: (*Laughing.*) The room is a mess. That one was a real fighter.

JOHN: He was a feisty fellow, wasn't he? The others all ran out before I had a chance to fire the gun. He's got to be the best one we've had.

AGNES: I agree, but I don't want to make a hasty decision. Come on, help me clean up this mess.

JOHN: I will as soon as I get some more blanks to reload the gun.

(BEN meets back at the office with MAXINE.)

MAXINE o.s.: (*Concerned.*) Ben, what happened? You look like you've been through a war.

BEN O.S.: I have. And the more I think about it, the angrier I get.

MAXINE O.S.: (*smugly.*) Does that mean you didn't get the listing?

BEN O.S.: Tell me, Maxine, how long have you been in real estate?

MAXINE O.S.: Five years.

BEN O.S.: And I'll bet you feel you've encountered almost every type of client possible, right?

MAXINE O.S.: I've handled some very difficult people.

BENO.S.: And you're thinking that I should have taken you along, like you suggested. Right?

MAXINE O. S.: Well, I don't like to brag, but yes. If you'd taken me along, you would have gotten the listing.

BEN O.S.: (*Raising his voice.*) And if I were to take you back there right now, you'd show me just how to do it?

MAXINE O.S.: Ben, what's gotten into you? I wouldn't dream of interfering with your client.

BEN O.S.: Oh, but I want you to. Come on, let's go.

MAXINE o.s.: You're taking me there now? I don't understand.

BEN o.s.: You will.

The Living Room is back in order again without the barricades. JOHN and AGNES Enter and sit down.)

AGNES: (*Looking around.*) Well, everything is back to normal.

(DOORBELL RINGS.)

JOHN: Someone's here. Did you call another agent?

AGNES: No. I can't imagine who it is. Take a look out the window.

(*JOHN looks out the window.*)

JOHN: (*Excited.*) Agnes, it's Ben. He came back and this time he's got a woman with him. Maybe he called the police on us. We did get a little carried away this time.

AGNES: Oh, John, that woman could be a plain-clothes detective here to arrest us.

(DOORBELL RINGS AGAIN.)

JOHN: Don't answer it. Maybe they'll go away.

AGNES: We have to answer it. Our car is in the driveway. They know we're in here. What are we going to do?

JOHN: I've got it. We'll pretend that we never saw this Ben guy before. We'll deny everything.

AGNES: Right. It's his word against ours.

(THE DOORBELL RINGS AGAIN.)

JOHN: I'll answer the door.

BEN O.S.: Hello, Mr. Bagley. I'm back. And this time I've brought someone with me, and I want you to tell her everything that happened here this afternoon.

JOHN (O.S.): Pardon me, sir. You must be mistaken. I don't know what you're talking about.

AGNES:(*Calling out.*) Who's at the door, sweetheart?

BEN (O.S.) That's his crazy wife. Come on, Maxine.

(*BEN enters dragging MAXINE along. JOHN is right behind them.*)

JOHN: Hey, wait a minute. You can't just barge into my house.

MAXINE: (*Nervously.*) Ben, are you sure this the right house?

AGNES: Who are you, young man? And what do you want?

JOHN: They just pushed right past me, Agnes.

BEN: (*Yelling.*) Where are the barricades?

JOHN: What barricades?

MAXINE: Really, Ben, maybe you've been working too hard. I think we'd better go.

BEN: No. We're not leaving until you hear the whole story. Go on Agnes, tell Maxine what a bum your husband is, and how he tried to shoot me.

AGNES: (*Shocked.*) My husband a bum? You must be insane. My John is he sweetest man there ever was.

45

BEN: Okay then, John, you tell her how Agnes only wanted to sell half the house and what a pain in the …

MAXINE: (*Interrupting.*) Ben! Please! Have you lost your mind? No wonder you can't get a listing when you barge into people's
homes and insult them.

JOHN: Yeah, you tell him, lady.

MAXINE: In all my years in real estate, I've never seen another agent act so badly.

AGNES: Years in real estate? Then you're not a policewoman?

BEN: Of course she's not...she's...oh, wait a minute. That's why you were pretending you'd never seen me before. You thought I called the cops on you. Well, you know what? That's a great idea. Where's the phone?

JOHN: (*Laughing nervously.*) Oh, come on, Ben. Can't you take a little joke? Agnes and I were just trying to find the toughest real estate agent in town to handle the sale of our house.

BEN: You mean the barricades, and all the fighting and shooting were just to see if I was tough?

AGNES: And you were, Ben. John and I both agreed you were the best agent we tested.

JOHN: So that's why we insist that you handle the sale of our house, the whole house of course.

MAXINE: (*Smugly.*) You see, Ben, I told you if I came along, you'd get the listing.

AGNES: Ben, I know we were a little rough on you, but please say you'll be our agent.

BEN: Nope!

MAXINE: No? Ben, be sensible. It's a lovely house. Any agent would be thrilled to get a listing like this.

46

JOHN: That's right. Any agent would jump at the chance to sell this house.

BEN: But any agent wasn't good enough for you two. You had to find the toughest agent in town.

AGNES: And we did. You. So why won't you take the listing?

BEN: Because I'm quitting real estate.

MAXINE: (*Shocked.*) Quitting? Ben, you just started a few weeks ago.

BEN: I know. I wanted a military career, but my family told me I didn't have what it takes to survive combat. Today I learned that I do have what it takes, so I am joining the Marines.

JOHN: That's wonderful, Ben. I was a Marine.

BEN: If you were a Marine. I think I will join the Navy.

The End

THE COUNT

This is a shortened version of the vampire skit that started my comedy writing career. It has a number of comic elements including the names of the characters and their family relationships.

The concept and story is outrageous, but it has proven to be a skit that gets laughs from beginning to end. What I like best about this skit is that the audience catches on to the interaction between the vampire and the census taker quickly and begins laughing in anticipation of the next laugh line.

Performing in this skit should be as much fun for the actors as it is for the audience. Pretend that vampires are real people and deliver the lines with sincerity.

The Count

Cast of Characters:

Count Down: Vampire Father

Countess Overbite: Vampire Mother

Miss Counted: Vampire Daughter

Count Me In: Vampire twin of Count Me Out

Kathy: Census Taker

At Rise: COUNT DOWN and COUNTESS OVERBITE are lounging on stage.

COUNT DOWN: Countess Overbite, go tell that daughter of yours to stop singing. She's going to wake up our neighbors in the cemetery.

COUNTESS OVERBITE: Miss Counted is practicing already? Well, no wonder! We've overslept. It's way past dark.

(There is a short scream and then a crash from off-stage. MISS COUNTED enters.)

MISS COUNTED: Mother, Count Me In is throwing things again.

COUNTESS OVERBITE: Count Down, I think you'd better have another vampire to vampire talk with your son. I'll send him in to see you.

(MISS COUNTED and COUNTESS OVERBITE exit. A few seconds later, COUNT ME IN enters.)

COUNT ME IN: He did it again! My loving twin brother left the house before dark while I was still sleeping.

COUNT DOWN: I don't think so. Count Me Out knows better than to venture out in the light. You just overslept.

COUNT ME IN: He could have woke me up. He never takes me with him anymore, but he lets that little twerp, Count One, Two, Three go everywhere with him.

COUNT DOWN: Oh....wait a minute. You're getting upset for nothing. He took Count One, Two, Three over to Wrigley Field. Don't you remember? I asked him to take your little brother to see the Cubs game.

COUNT ME IN: So big deal. After all these years, the Cubs are playing night games. Count One, Two, Three still isn't going to get to be a bat boy. He's a hundred and three years old. They only hire kids.

COUNT DOWN: Must I constantly remind you that the passing of time has no effect on us. We are eternally young in body and mind.

(MISS COUNTED and COUNTESS OVERBITE enter.)

MISS COUNTED: Mother said I could cook breakfast. Do you want your plasma boiled, scrambled, or sunny-side up?

COUNT ME IN: Oh, yuk! If she's cooking, I'm not eating.

COUNT DOWN: Why eat in tonight? We can all go out for a bite.

COUNTESS OVERBITE: What a wonderful idea.   I've had a taste for some AB negative for weeks now.

MISS COUNTED: I can't go out. I don't have a thing to wear.

COUNT ME IN: Oh go on, Miss Counted. You always look like a million bucks......all dirty and wrinkled.

MISS COUNTED: Mother! Make him apologize!

(*Loud knocking on the door.*)

COUNTESS OVERBITE: Someone's at the door. How wonderful! Count Me In, you answer it, while the rest of us dress for our night on the town.

(*COUNT DOWN, COUNTESS OVERBITE AND MISS COUNTED exit. COUNT ME IN goes to the door and returns a few seconds later with Kathy carrying a clipboard and pen.*)

KATHY: I'm sorry if I disturbed your sleep, but I've been here twice during the day, and haven't been able to rouse anyone. Do you work nights?

COUNT ME IN: You might say that. But don't worry your pretty little neck...eh I mean head about that. Please sit down.

(*COUNT ME IN pulls out a chair for her. She sits down, and then he pulls the other chair very close to her and sits down on it.*)

KATHY: (*Nervously.*) As I told you at the door, I'm from the census bureau and I need information on all the people who live here. Why don't we start with you? Your name please.

COUNT ME IN: Count Me In.

KATHY: Yes, I will. That's what we census takers get paid to do, count people. Now may I have your name, please?

COUNT ME IN: Count Me In.

KATHY: I said I would. Maybe you don't understand. Let's go on to the next question. Do you have any brothers?

COUNT ME IN: Count Me Out.

KATHY: Oh, I can't do that, I've already counted you in. Whatever your name is.

COUNT ME IN: Count Me In.

KATHY: I wish you'd make up your mind. I don't have all night. Now about your brother...

COUNT ME IN: Count Me Out.

KATHY: (Annoyed.) Now stop it. First you're in, then you're out.

COUNT ME IN: Honey, I'm always In. It's my brother who's out.

KATHY: Never mind. Next question, do you have any other brothers?

COUNT ME IN: Count One, Two, Three.

KATHY: Good. Now we're getting somewhere. One, two, three, plus you, makes four boys. Any girls?

COUNT ME IN: Miss Counted.

KATHY: (Indignant.) Really sir, I am an official census taker. We never miscount. The government depends on our accuracy. Oh....you got me so confused I forgot to get the last name of your family. What is it?

COUNT ME IN: Dracula.

KATHY: (Laughing.) Dracula...very funny. Next you'll tell me you're a vampire.

COUNT ME IN: That's right, sweetheart, and you've got the prettiest neck I've seen in years. How about a little bite?

(*COUNT ME IN lunges at her. KATHY jumps up and runs, but he grabs hold of her. To fend him off, KATHY stabs him in the chest with her pen. COUNT ME IN moans and falls to the floor.*)

KATHY: Oh, sir, I'm really sorry. I didn't realize my pen was so sharp.

(*KATHY bends over him, and COUNT ME IN, grabs her and bites her neck. She faints. With KATHY out, COUNT ME IN stands up clutching the pen in his chest. COUNT DOWN and COUNTESS OVERBITE enter.*)

COUNT DOWN: What's going on in here?

(COUNT ME IN points at KATHY)

COUNT ME IN: She flicked her Bic at me.

COUNTESS OVERBITE: Really, son, I've heard of writing from the heart, but this is ridiculous.

COUNT DOWN: There's some pliers in the basement next to the extra coffin. Go downstairs and pull that out.

COUNTESS OVERBITE: Pull it out carefully, dear. I don't want you to get ink on your clothes.

(*COUNT ME IN exits. COUNT DOWN and his wife walk over and look down at KATHY.*)

COUNT DOWN: Congratulations, Countess. It's a girl.

COUNTESS OVERBITE: Miss Counted will be so pleased to have a baby sister at last.

COUNT DOWN: It used to be so lonely when it was just the two of us in this big old house. Then, the government started sending these children to brighten our lives.

COUNTESS OVERBITE: Yes, Count, but it's such a pity.

COUNT DOWN: A pity? Why do you say that, love bite?

COUNTESS OVERBITE: Because now we have to wait another ten years for a visitor.

The End

Grandma is a Gangster

A young man introducing his girlfriend to his grandma should be a normal event, but in order to be comical, writers have to give it a unexpected twist.

In this skit, grandma is more than a little crazy. Read through this skit and identify the laugh lines. Then, rewrite the skit giving it your own twist. Maybe you would want grandma to be sane and the girlfriend to be crazy. Or put these characters in another situation. It is up to you. The main thing is to create your own script with these characters or ones of your own. All I am doing is giving you a basic format to get you started. This is not a test. It is just a suggestion.

If you do write your own version, have your friends or classmates perform it for you. Listening to other people read your work aloud is the best way to determine how it works.

If you want to create totally different characters, you can jump start the process by looking through magazines or newspaper ads to get ideas of how your character might look. Once the character is in your mind's eye, he/she will help you move forward.

The key to performing this skit as is requires an actor to accept the insanity of an old lady who thinks everything on television is part of her own persona. Grandma rules the comedy in this skit and the boy and girl just have to react to her craziness.

Grandma is a Gangster

Cast of Characters:

GRANDMA: Eccentric Older Woman

BILLY: her grandson

JANE: Billy's girlfriend

UNCLE JOE: Grandma's son

SET: Living room with a few chairs and a small table

PROPS: Gun for Grandma and rope.

AT RISE: *GRANDMA is seated in a chair, holding her gun in her lap. BILLY AND JANE enter.*

GRANDMA: Who let you varmints in here?

BILLY: No one. the door was open. It's me, Billy.

(*GRANDMA points the gun at them.*)

GRANDMA: I've been waiting for you, kid. Get your hands up.

BILLY: I'm Billy, your grandson, not Billy the Kid.

GRANDMA: Prove it.

BILLY: Your name is Ida Mae, You were married to Arnold Goat on February 14th.

GRANDMA: Valentine's Day, same day as the massacre. That's why Big Al couldn't come to our wedding.

BILLY: Put the gun down, Grandma. I came over here to introduce you to my girlfriend. This is Jane. Jane, this is my dad's mother, Ida Mae.

JANE: It's nice to meet you. How are you doing today?

(*JANE walks past GRANDMA and looks around. GRANDMA jumps up and sticks her gun in JANE'S back.*)

GRANDMA: I'm doing just fine, girlie. And if you want to live to be as old as I am, never turn your back on a gun.

(*JANE freezes in fright. BILLY hurries forward and grabs the gun, lowering it away from JANE.*)

BILLY: Cut it out, Grandma. Sit down and behave. (*He turns to Jane.*) Don't worry, the gun isn't real. Grandma is just hooked on gangster and cowboy movies. Since Uncle Joe got her NetFlix all she does is watch old westerns and gangster movies.

(*GRANDMA sits down again, but keeps her gun pointed at them.*)

JANE: Is that the way she greets all her visitors?

BILLY: No. My Uncle Joe lives here and usually keeps her in line. (*He turns to GRANDMA.*) Where's Uncle Joe, Grandma?

GRANDMA: Who's that?

BILLY: Your youngest son. The one who lives with you, and likes beer and pretzels.

GRANDMA: Oh, you mean Bugsy. He's tied up today, but you two can sit down and wait for him.

BILLY: Sure. I want Jane to meet him too.

(*BILLY AND JANE sit down in the other chairs.*)

JANE: You have a very nice house.

GRANDMA: It's a front for the speakeasy in the basement.

BILLY: She's kidding. The only thing in the basement is an old washing machine.

GRANDMA: That's where we hide the gin when the cops show up.

JANE: Oh, I thought maybe that's where you laundered the cash.

(*GRANDMA points her gun at JANE again.*)

GRANDMA: Shut your pie hole, girl, or you'll end up swimming with the fish.

BILLY: Jane is kidding, Grandma, and you need to mind your manners.

GRANDMA: Okay. Are you hungry? I got some good grub in the kitchen.

JANE: What's on the menu?

GRANDMA: Spaghetti and beans. I call it Capone on the Range. They wrote a song about it.

BILLY: No, thanks. I came over to tell you some good news. Jane and I are getting married.

GRANDMA: Does your parole officer know about this?

JANE: (*To Billy.*) You're on parole?

BILLY: Of course not. I've never even been arrested, except once for a traffic ticket.

GRANDMA: I bribed the Judge and he beat the rap.

BILLY: Stop it, Grandma. I came here to give you good news and you're acting crazy.

GRANDMA: I'll be happy for you, after I get a few answers from Calamity Jane here.

JANE: That's fine. What would you like to know?

GRANDMA: What's your family name?

JANE: James.

GRANDMA: Is your father still in banking?

JANE: He is.

GRANDMA: Hot Dog. I'll bet he's still making withdrawals on a regular basis. You tell your daddy, Ida Mae says, hey.

(*Jane turns to Billy in confusion.*)

JANE: She knows my father?

BILLY: (*Shaking his head.*) Grandma, Jane's father is not a bank robber. He's the President of a bank.

JANE: Oh, I get it. Because my last name is James, she thinks my father is Jessie James. That's hysterical.

(JANE begins to laugh. GRANDMA points her gun at Jane again.)

GRANDMA: No one laughs at Ida Mae Goat and lives to tell about it.

BILLY: That's it. We're leaving.

(He pulls JANE to her feet)

GRANDMA: Okay. I'll let you leave, but if you tell anyone about me and my hideout, you'll both be wearing cement shoes.

BILLY: I'm going to have my dad call Uncle Joe, and tell him to cancel your NetFlix subscription.

GRANDMA: Who's your dad going to call?

BILLY: Bugsy. My dad will call Bugsy.

GRANDMA: You can tell Bugsy yourself... Hey, Bugsy, get out here. Bonnie and Clyde want to talk to you.

(UNCLE JOE comes hopping onto the stage with legs and arms tied up with rope. Jane and Billy stare at him.)

GRANDMA: I told you he was tied up.

The End

Back with the Breeze
Sequel to Gone with the Wind

This skit is a parody. That is a humorous imitation of a serious work of literature. In this case, I am making fun of the classic novel/movie, <u>Gone with the Wind</u>.

The main character is named Red instead Scarlet. Instead of running a plantation she is running for a political office. The situation and interaction of the characters are twisted similarities of the original novel. The same is true of the dialogue.

Since a parody is an accepted venue for comedy, writers reading this book should create their own parody based on a novel or film. However, the original work has to be popular or well-known enough for people to recognize the humor in it. I also suggest that you limit the cast as I did in this skit.

Performing this skit requires a female who likes to scream, and heroine who has the wit and nerve of the woman in the novel. The same goes for the male lead.

<u>Back with the Breeze</u>

<u>Cast of Characters</u>:

Red O'Meara

Mollie

Jack

Set: Hotel Suite with chairs and a desk.

Props: book, telephone, brown bag with carrot, doll, wrapped package with hard hat

At rise: RED is at the desk, talking on the telephone

RED: Now you listen to me, Sissy. I promised Humphrey I would take care of Mollie while he was on tour. And you promised to help me......I don't care how much they're paying you to be on that show...Oh? well sure, I know who he is. You tell him I said, Hey.

(A scream from O.S.)

Yes, that was Mollie yelling.
Apparently being in labor hurts....Okay, I'll tell her. Bye now.

(RED hangs up as another scream is heard from O.S.)

RED: Stop your screaming, Mollie. Sissy heard you all the way in California.

(RED sits in a chair, as a very pregnant MOLLIE waddles in and struggles to sit down too.)

MOLLIE: Is Sissy sorry she can't be here to help me birth this baby?

RED: Of course, she is. Sissy would much rather be here listening to you yell and carry on than be in California with movie stars. So, your labor has started?

MOLLIE: Not yet.

RED: Then why were you screaming?

MOLLIE: Humphrey called me on my cell phone to see how I was doing. It's part of the guilt trip I'm going to keep him on for the next three years.

RED: But you told him to go on this tour, didn't you?

MOLLIE: Yes, but he should have known I didn't mean it, and stayed with me.

RED: I know what you mean. I told Jack Butler to get out of my life, and he left me at the altar.

MOLLIE: Well, you're doing fine without him. Oh, Red, you're so cool to take time off from campaigning to take care of me.

(MOLLIE lets out a cry and doubles over in pain)

RED: What's wrong?

MOLLIE: (Still in pain.) The baby...oh, Red. I'm going to have Humphrey's baby right here.

RED: You'd better go into the bedroom and lie down. I'll call someone.

(MOLLIE exits as Red goes to the telephone.)

RED: Hello, room service? I want to order lunch. Emergencies always make me so hungry...What do you mean, the kitchen is closed?....All right, then, send a doctor up here.

(MOLLIE screams from off-stage.)

RED: And make it fast.

(RED hangs up the phone and reaches under the desk and pulls out a brown bag and takes out a carrot.)

RED: Are you hungry, Mollie?

(MOLLIE screams again O.S.)

RED: (*Shrugging.*) I guess not. (*Looking at the carrot.*) You can never count on room service, and when I left the farm, I swore I'd never go hungry again.

MOLLIE O.S.: Red, is the doctor here yet?

RED: Not yet. You'll have to hang on, Mollie. Think about something else, like the way the spotlight bounces off Humphrey's gold Lemay suit.

(MOLLIE screams again. RED is about to take a bite of the carrot, but there is a knock on the door. Red drops the carrot and goes to answer it. JACK BUTLER enters carrying a book and a wrapped package.)

JACK: So, Red, we meet again.

RED: Jack Butler, I heard you were back in New York. You certainly took your sweet time coming to see me.

JACK: I wanted to give you time to miss me.
RED: I heard they banned you from Las Vegas again.

JACK: Yes, and it's been wonderful publicity for my book. I brought you an autographed copy.

(*JACK hands RED the book and she reads the title.*)

RED: Frankly, I don't give a damn, and that's why I'm a winner.

(MOLLIE screams O.S.)

JACK: (*Motioning towards the bedroom.*) Would you mind turning the radio off, Red? You know I don't like Humphrey's singing.

RED: (*Indignant.*) Don't you dare come in here and insult Humphrey.

JACK: That's what I like about you, Red. You're a woman who knows what she wants. Too bad he married someone else.

RED: (*Pouting.*) Stop it. Can't you see I'm upset? Mollie needs a doctor. She's in my bedroom having Humphrey's baby. At least he knows how to make a woman happy.

(*MOLLIE screams from O.S.*)

JACK: Yes, I can tell she's ecstatic! Where's Sissy? I thought she was with you.

RED: Oh, I can't count on her anymore. Ever since they gave her that talk show in Chicago, she's been impossible.

JACK: I brought you a gift. Open it while we're waiting for the doctor.

(*JACK hands her a wrapped package. She opens it to find a hard hat.*)

RED: It's very nice, Jack. I can wear it Friday night when I speak to the teamsters.

JACK: It's not for your campaign speeches. It's for Humphrey's next concert. Look inside. It's got built-in ear plugs.

(*RED throws the hat onto a chair.*)

RED: You're just jealous because Humphrey is idolized by millions.

JACK: No, my darling. I'm jealous because he's idolized by you. I've waited a long time for you Red, longer than I've waited for a bus on Fifth Avenue.

(JACK tries to hug RED.)

MOLLIE O.S.: (*Yelling.*) The baby's coming. I can feel it.

RED: Let go of me, Jack. We have to help Mollie.

(*The telephone rings. RED goes to answer it. JACK runs off stage to help MOLLIE.*)

RED: Hello. Oh, Humphrey, Humphrey, how wonderful to hear your voice.......Mollie? Yes, she's here. You want to speak to her?

(*MOLLIE screams O.S.*)

JACK O.S.: Hurry, Red!!

RED: (*Still on phone.*) Eh....Humphrey, darlin', we're kind of busy right now. I'll have Mollie call you back.

(*RED hangs up the phone and runs off stage. MOLLIE screams again. Then, JACK screams and then, a baby cries. JACK enters and falls into a chair.*)

JACK: It's a boy. He looks just like his mother.

(Baby cries again O.S.)

And he sounds just like his father.

(*RED enters carrying the baby.*)

RED: Why, Jack, I'm stunned. For the first time, I'm seeing you in a different light. You are the right man for me after all.

JACK: At last. Kiss me, Red.

RED: Not now. I must call the party....I can see it all now. You and me on the convention floor with the balloons and the posters....
O'Meara and Butler. (She raises the baby in the air) The team that delivers!

JACK: Convention? Posters?

RED: It'll be so exciting, me the presidential candidate and you my running mate. Oh, Jack, I have the perfect slogan for you.....Elect the vice, who knows how to roll the dice!

JACK: Forget it, Red. I'll not be a pawn in your political games. Good-bye.

(JACK exits. RED shrugs and speaks to the audience.)

RED: Oh, Fiddely dee.....I'll get him back. I'll return to the campaign trail. For tomorrow is not just another day, it's election day......and when I win the primary....

The End

NO LAUGHING MATTER
A One Act Comedy

This script is more of a short one act play than a skit. I wrote this for a high school drama teacher who asked for a script with enough characters for the number of students in his class.

The comedy elements in this script are the characters and the storyline which takes them from a classroom to a court room because of a post hypnotic suggestion. There are lots of laugh lines and examples of set up and delivery.

You will notice that the format of this script is different from the others in this book. While there are no hard and fast rules for formatting stage plays, most publishers use the format in the first nine scripts in this book. However, the format for No Laughing Matter is required for screenplays and TV scripts, but acceptable for stage plays too.

Performers for No Laughing Matter must be aware of all the other characters in each setting and allow pauses between their lines and the others who are delivering laugh lines.

Whenever you are performing comedy, be aware that you need to give the audience time to react to the laugh lines. Also, be aware that if you are enjoying yourself in a comedy, the audience will enjoy it too.

No Laughing Matter

Cast of Characters

Benny Gardner: (male) very smug attorney

Wilma Gardner: (female) Benny's younger sister

Duane: (male) Wilma's boyfriend

Marian: (female) Duane's sister

Miller: (male or female) teacher

Ida: (female) middle aged woman

Arnold: (male) Ida's husband

Bob: (male) young student

Grandpa: (male) Bob's elderly relative

Denise: (female)another student

Cop

Bailiff

Judge

SCENE 1

WILMA

Hi, I'm Wilma. I never thought I'd be in front of an audience, but my brother talked me into it. He thinks everyone should hear our story.

(BENNY SMILES AND WAVES TO THE AUDIENCE)

BENNY

It's a great story.

WILMA

This is my brother, Benny. He's an attorney. Now before you get too impressed, let me tell you Benny's success rate in the court room had been less than spectacular. His law office is a desk in the corner of the basement, where he drums up clients by listening to the police calls on his special radio.

BENNY

Someone has to help those poor people.

WILMA

Right. Anyway…It seems no reputable law firm wants to hire Benny because he earned a reputation for eccentric behavior. In other words, Benny is a jerk.

BENNY

(Insulted)

Hey!

WILMA

But I love him anyway.

BENNY

(Smiling)

That's better.

WILMA

The other important people in my life are my boyfriend Duane and his sister, Marian.

DUANE

Wilma and I are getting married as soon as I finish school. I'm studying to be a minister.

BENNY

Big deal. Law school is much harder.

MARIAN

Is that why it took you so long to graduate?

WILMA

That's Marian. She's Duane's sister. Benny has been in love
with her for years, but she would never go out with him because she thinks he weird.

DUANE

Everyone thinks Benny is weird.

BENNY

Listen up, people. I don't have to stand out here and be insulted.

MARIAN

That's right, Benny. You can be insulted anywhere, and you usually are.

WILMA

Maybe you all better wait backstage, so I can get on with the story.

MARIAN

Good idea. These lights are making my hair frizz.

BENNY

I for one, like frizzy. Nothing like cuddling up with a Brillo pad.

MIRIAN

Oh!

WILMA

Okay, it all started because I needed a favor. After meeting Benny, you would think that he would be the last person I'd ask me to help me with a problem. You're right. He was my last choice, he wasn't exactly anxious to help me out. Here's how it all happened.

WE MOVE ON TO A TYPICAL SCHOOL CLASSROOM. SEATED AT THE DESKS ARE IDA, ARNOLD, DENISE, JACKIE, BOB AND BOB'S GRANDPA.
WILMA AND BENNY ENTER AND STAND OFF TO ONE SIDE AS BENNY LOOKS THINGS OVER.

BENNY

I changed my mind, Wilma. I can't do this.

WILMA

One tiny favor, that's all I'm asking for.

BENNY

It's not a tiny favor. Otherwise you could
have talked some other sap into doing it.
Speaking of saps where's Duane? You can
talk him into anything.

WILMA

Duane is studying for an important exam
tomorrow. Marian has a date, and Jack
hung up on me.

BENNY

I know, he told me. Let's get out of here,
Wilma. I wouldn't be a good subject for
your hypnotism class anyway. I'm an
attorney, a take-charge kind of guy. There's
no way I could be hypnotized.

WILMA

Please, Benny, tonight's the last night of my
class. I promised to bring somebody to
hypnotize. If you don't do it, I'll be
embarrassed in front of the whole class.

BENNY

So? It wouldn't be the first time.

WILMA

All right, Benny. What if I get Marian to go
to the dance with you next week? That way
you don't have to call all those phone
numbers on the wall in the bus station.

BENNY

Are you sure you can get her to go with me?

WILMA
She owes me a big favor.

BENNY
Well, okay. In that case, I'll be glad to help
you out, sis.

HENRY MILLER ENTERS THE CLASSROOM PASSING BY WILMA AND
BENNY. BENNY LOOKS SURPRISED TO SEE HIM AND GRABS
WILMA'S ARM.

BENNY
Hey, see that guy that just came in?

HE POINTS TO HENRY MILLER WHO IS TALKING TO THE
STUDENTS WHO ARE ALREADY SEATED.

WILMA
Yeah. Why?

BENNY
That crook is in your class?

WILMA
No, he is not in my class. And why are you
calling the man a crook?

BENNY
Because he is one. I've waited years to catch
up with that two-bit, cheap, con-artist.

WILMA
 (Upset)
Oh no! you're not going to come in my class
and make a scene are you?

BENNY
A scene? Wilma that man is a fugitive. He
jumped bail and I lost two thousand dollars.
I'm going to call the police and turn him in.
Maybe there's a reward.

MILLER TURNS AROUND AND WAVES AT WILMA. BENNY HIDES
BEHIND HER.

MILLER
Wilma, we're waiting for you and your
guest.

WILMA
(Calling out)
We'll be right there Mr. Miller.

MILLER TURNS BACK TO THE OTHER STUDENTS.

BENNY
I thought you said he wasn't in your class.

WILMA
He's not in the class. He's teaching the class.

BENNY
Okay, fine. At least I know he'll be here
when the police show up to nab him.

WILMA
You can't have him arrested in front of the
whole class.

BENNY

Why not? But wait a minute, I can't let him
see me. He might recognize me and take off.
Wilma, you'll have to stall for a few minutes.

WILMA

But, Benny, I'm supposed to be bringing a
subject to be hypnotized. I promised the
class.

BENNY

Don't worry. I'll be there in a few minutes.
And when I come in, you just take my lead.

BENNY GIVES WILMA A LITTLE SHOVE AND SHE WALKS OVER TO
THE OTHER STUDENTS AND TAKES A SEAT. IDA, ONE OF THE
STUDENTS, STANDS UP TO SPEAK.

IDA

Good evening, everybody. I'm really excited
about tonight's class. The finale you might
say. Anyway, I brought my husband,
Arnold, along to be hypnotized. Stand up,
Arnie.

ARNOLD ATTEMPTS TO STAND AS HIS WIFE HAS REQUESTED.
HOWEVER, HE CANNOT EXTRICATE HIMSELF FROM UNDER THE
DESKTOP. HE STRUGGLES AND THEN STANDS PICKING UP THE
ENTIRE DESK WITH HIM.

ARNOLD

Good evening... I seem to be stuck in this
contraption... Excuse me, please.

THE REST OF THE CLASS SMILES INDULGENTLY AT ARNOLD.
WILMA IS IN HER SEAT LOOKING NERVOUSLY TOWARDS THE
DOOR. DENISE GETS UP.

DENISE
This is my sister, Jackie. Stand up Jackie.

JACKIE
Hi. Nice to meet you all. I'm not taking my clothes off.

DENISE
No one asked you to.

JACKIE
That old man over there did.

JACKIE POINTS TO BOB'S GRANDPA.

MILLER
That's Bob's guest. I'm sure he was just kidding.

BOB STANDS IN RESPONSE TO HIS NAME. HE POKES THE MAN NEXT TO HIM, A FEISTY GENTLEMAN IN HIS EIGHTIES.

GRANDPA
It never hurts to ask.

BOB
(Embarrassed)
Nobody in my family wanted to be hypnotized, so I brought my grandfather. He'll do anything to get out of the house, and don't worry, he's harmless.

GRANDPA
Speak for yourself, sonny.

77

MILLER
(Looking at Wilma)
Wilma, where's your guest? Didn't I see you
with a gentleman?

WILMA
Eh… yes, sir, you did. But he had to leave,
so…eh…just carry on.

BENNY ENTERS AGAIN, ONLY NOW HE IS DRESSED LIKE A BIKER.
COMPLETE WITH BOOTS, BLACK LEATHER JACKET, LOTS OF GOLD
CHAINS AND A PAIR OF DARK GLASSES.

BENNY
Here I am, Sis. You didn't think I'd let you
down. Hey, everybody, I'm Flash, Wilma's
older, but very charming brother.

WILMA IS SHOCKED BUT DOESN'T SAY ANYTHING. MILLER WALKS
OVER AND EXTENDS HIS HAND TO BENNY.

MILLER
Good evening. We're happy you could join
us.

BENNY SLAPS HIS HAND IN A GREETING AND TWIRLS AROUND AND
SLIDES INTO THE SEAT NEXT TO WILMA.

BENNY
Let the show begin, brother!!

MILLER WALKS BACK TO THE FRONT OF THE CLASS. WILMA
LEANS OVER TO TALK TO BENNY.

WILMA
(Whispering)
Where did you get those awful clothes?

BENNY
(Whispering back)
Some guy I met outside by the telephone
rented them to me.

WILMA
This is humiliating. I think we should leave.

BENNY
(Urgently)
No way. A cop is on his way to arrest this
crook.

WILMA GASPS AND COVERS HER MOUTH

MILLER
All right. It seems that everyone is here.
Let's begin our journey into sub-conscious.
The purpose
of this exercise is to let you students observe
the techniques of hypnotism and the actions
of hypnotized subjects. May I have all the
volunteers up front next to me, please.

ARNOLD, BENNY, GRANDPA AND JACKIE RISE FROM THEIR SEATS
AND GO UP TO THE FRONT OF THE ROOM TO SIT IN THE CHAIRS
LINED UP FOR THEM.

BENNY
Say, brother, what if you can't hypnotize us?
Like some of us may not fall under your
spell.

MILLER
That's not likely. However, if it should
happen that person would be excused from
the demonstration.

BENNY NODS AND TAKES HIS PLACE WITH THE OTHERS. MILLER
FACES THEM AND REMOVES A CRYSTAL ON A SILVER CHAIN FROM
HIS JACKET POCKET. HE BEGINS TO SWING THE CRYSTAL BACK
AND FORTH IN FRONT OF THE FOUR SUBJECTS.

MILLER
(Continuing)
Concentrate on the sparkling beauty of the
crystal. Notice how it catches the light and
absorbs the colors around it. Now imagine
your mind as the crystal. You are absorbing
the sound of my voice. All other sights and
sounds are non-existent. You hear only the
sound of my voice. You are feeling relaxed
as my voice protects you.
You will sleep now and hear only the sound
of my voice as it guides you deeper and
deeper into sleep…
sleep… sleep.

ONE BY ONE EACH OF THE SUBJECTS FALLS UNDER HIS HYPNOTIC
SPELL INCLUDING BENNY. MILLER WALKS BY EACH OF THEM AND
RAISES ONE HAND AND LETS IT DROP LIMPLY INTO THEIR LAPS AS
HE VERIFIES THAT THEY ARE IN A TRANCE.

IDA
Do hypnotized people always tell the truth?

MILLER
Yes, they do.

IDA

Good. Ask Arnie how he feels about the new
secretary he hired.

MILLER

Arnold, can you hear me?

ARNOLD

Yes. I hear you.

MILLER

How do you feel about the new secretary
you hired?

ARNIE LETS OUT A WOLF WHISTLE AND GESTURES WITH HIS
HANDS SHE IS VERY SHAPELY.

IDA

That's it! Tomorrow you fire her!

MILLER STEPS BETWEEN ARNIE AND IDA AS SHE WAVES HER
HANDBAG, THREATENING ARNOLD.

MILLER

Please, Ida, let me ask Arnie another
question. Arnold, do you love your wife?

ARNOLD

(Smiling)
Yes.

MILLER

And is there any reason your wife should be
jealous of your new secretary?

ARNOLD
No. Ida is the only woman for me.

MILLER
Well, now that we've saved a marriage and a
job, let's move on with the demonstration. I
will now direct the subjects as a group
through a few simple questions.
  (pause for effect)

You are no longer people sitting in chairs.
You have become chickens, and will remain
chickens until you hear the words that strike
fear in the hearts of chickens everywhere.

IMMEDIATELY, THE FOUR SUBJECTS RISE FROM THEIR CHAIRS
AND START DASHING AROUND LIKE CHICKENS, CLUCKING,
FLAPPING THEIR WINGS AND PECKING AT ONE ANOTHER.
GRANDPA IS CHASING JACKIE.

MILLER
(Yelling)
Colonel Sanders!

WITH FINAL FRIGHTENING SQUAWKS, THE SUBJECTS RUSH BACK
TO THEIR CHAIRS AND BECOME PEOPLE AGAIN.

JACKIE
That old rooster was trying to pluck my
feathers!

DENISE
Are you bragging or complaining?

MILLER
Sleep… Sleep…

IMMEDIATELY, THE SUBJECTS RELAX AGAIN.

>   DENISE
> Mr. Miller, last week you talked about post-
> hypnotic suggestions. Can you show us how
> that works?

>   MILLER
> Yes, as a matter of fact. That is the next part
> of this demonstration. I will give a suggestion
> that will be carried
> out before the end of class this evening.
>
> Listen carefully, on the count of three, I will
> clap my hands and you will awake and
> return to your places in the classroom. You
> will feel refreshed and happy. You will be as
> carefree as children. You will be so carefree
> that when you hear the word recess, you will
> start to laugh and be unable to stop until you
> hear the words.

A POLICEMAN ENTERS THE CLASSROOM. MILLER STOPS. HE IS
SHOCKED TO SEE HIM AND BACKS AWAY FROM HIS HYPNOTIZED
SUBJECTS.

>   MILLER
> Dear Lord…

>   COP
> Sorry to disturb you sir. I'm looking for a
> robbery suspect.

>   MILLER
> A robbery subject?

WILMA RUSHES FORWARD.

> WILMA
> Oh, Mr. Miller, I'm so sorry.

> COP
> (Cop looks curiously at the hypnotized
> subjects)
> What's going on here?

> WILMA
> They're hypnotized, and before you take
> Mr. Miller to the slammer, he's got to wake
> them up.

> MILLER
> (Very nervously)
> The slammer? Wilma, what in the world
> are you talking about?

> WILMA
> Eh…well…wake them up first and then I'll
> tell you.

> MILLER
> One, Two, Three….

MILLER CLAPS HIS HANDS AND THE FOUR SUBJECTS INSTANTLY
AWAKE, AND LOOK AROUND SLIGHTLY BEWILDERED. THE COP
WALKS OVER TO BENNY.

> COP
> The rest of you people can leave. I've got my
> man.

BENNY
Good work, although you sure took your
sweet time getting here.

EVERYONE EXITS EXCEPT WILMA, BENNY AND THE COP.

BENNY
Hey, he's getting away! Arrest him!

BENNY TRIES TO WALK FORWARD BUT THE COP PUTS HANDCUFFS
ON HIM AND STARTS TO READ HIM HIS RIGHTS.

COP
You have the right to remain silent.
Anything you…

BENNY
Are you crazy? I'm not the one you're
supposed to arrest. I'm the one who called
you.

WILMA TRIES TO GET BETWEEN BENNY AND THE POLICEMEN.

WILMA
Get your hands off my brother. He called
you to arrest Mr. Miller.

COP
Get out of my way lady….

BENNY
You are making a big mistake. I'm a lawyer.
I recognized this conman from a couple of
years ago and called the cops to have him
arrested. You're letting him get away.

                    WILMA
          (Yelling at policeman)
          Quit harassing my brother, and get out
          there and get the real
          crook.

                    COP
          Are you with this guy?

                    WILMA
          Yes.

                    COP
          You must be an accomplice!

THE NEXT MORNING.

THE COP ENTERS WITH WILMA AND BENNY. THEY ARE NO
LONGER HANDCUFFED. THEY STOP IN THE MIDDLE OF THE ROOM
SO THEY CAN TALK.

                    WILMA
          (Angrily)
          We're being taken into the courtroom,
          Benny.

                    BENNY
          Don't worry, it's standard procedure.

                    WILMA
          But you said we'd never get to court because
          the police don't want anyone to know about
          the stupid mistakes they make.
          You said you'd have us out of jail in ten
          minutes. You said-

BENNY
Knock it off Wilma. I'm working on our
defense.

WILMA
(slowly and fearfully)
Our defense? I knew it. I'm going to spend
the rest of my life in jail. Duane will marry
someone else. And all because you wanted
to arrest Mr. Miller for something that
happened years ago.

THE COP ESCORTS WILMA AND BENNY TO THEIR TABLE IN THE
COURTROOM. DUANE AND MARIAN ENTER AND RUSH OVER TO
BENNY AND WILMA.

DUANE
Wilma, are you all right?

WILMA JUMPS UP AND THROWS HER ARMS AROUND DUANE. HE
COMFORTS HER.

MARIAN
We came over as soon as we heard. What
can we do to help?

BENNY
Nothing. I've got everything under control.

DUANE
I think you need a good lawyer.

BENNY
May I remind you that I am a lawyer?

MARIAN

You don't have to remind me. I'm still
paying for that traffic ticket you helped me
with.

DUANE

Seriously, Benny, do you think it's a good
idea to represent
yourself? You know what they say, a man
who represents himself, has a fool for a
client.

MARIAN

Forget that argument, Duane. Being a fool
never stopped Benny before.

WILMA

Oh, Duane, if I go to jail will you wait for
me?

DUANE

You're not going to jail, Wilma. No one
could possibly believe
that you committed a crime.

WILMA

But what about Benny? Two women, who
witnessed the robbery, picked
Benny out of the lineup.

BENNY

No problem. Once they find out who I really
am, those women will realize that choosing
me was a dumb mistake.

MARIAN

Benny's right Wilma. Every woman that's
ever gone out with him has come to the
same conclusion

BENNY

(Sarcastically)

I'm so glad you came down here to give us
moral support. You can run along now. I
wouldn't want you to miss the auditions for
Saturday Night Live!

DUANE

Oh, come on, Benny. You know we're
behind you one hundred per cent.

MARIAN

We're just making jokes to try to cheer you
up.

BENNY

Well, excuse me for not laughing.

BAILIFF

All rise. The Honorable Judge Callahan
presiding.

WILMA

Callahan? Benny, isn't she the Judge who
doesn't like you?

BENNY

Stop worrying, Wilma. Callahan doesn't
have to like me to dismiss the case.

WILMA BURIES HER FACE IN HER HANDS. CALLAHAN READS THE
PAPERS THE BAILIFF HANDS HIM AND THEN LOOKS UP TO SPEAK
TO BENNY AND WILMA.

                    CALLAHAN
          Mr. Gardner, it seems that you and your
          sister are accused of holding up a liquor
          store. How do you plead?

                    BENNY
          Not guilty, Your Honor. And if it please the
          court, I would like to dispense with the usual
          formalities. If Your Honor would
          grant me a few minutes to confer with him
          in his chambers, I'm sure we can clear up
          this matter very quickly.

                    CALLAHAN
          Since you are an attorney, known to this
          court, I will grant your
          request. But I warn you Gardner, this is a
          serious matter and I'll
          have none of your theatrical displays of
          humor.

                    BENNY
          Believe me, Your Honor. I realize the
          severity of the charges and my only desire is
          to clear them up in an expedient manner.

                    CALLAHAN
          Very well. Proceed to my chambers. This
          court stands in recess.

RESPONDING TO THE POST-HYPNOTIC SUGGESTION HE RECEIVED
EARLIER, WHEN BENNY HEARS THE WORD RECESS, HE BEGINS TO
LAUGH.

                    WILMA
        Benny, what's wrong with you? Stop
        laughing!

SHE LOOKS UP AT CALLAHAN WHO IS NOW GLARING AT BOTH OF
THEM.

                    CALLAHAN
        Mr. Gardner, I am going to cite you for
        contempt.

                    MARIAN
        A good laugh is worth two hours sleep. And
        at the rate Benny is going, he'll be awake for
        a week.

                    DUANE
        If he doesn't stop laughing like a hyena, he'll
        spend that week behind bars. What could
        have caused him to break up like this?

                    MARIAN
        Maybe it's a delayed reaction to our jokes.

BENNY IS NOW ROLLING AROUND ON THE FLOOR LAUGHING
UNCONTROLLABLY. WILMA REALIZES WHY BENNY IS LAUGHING.

                    WILMA
        Oh, Your Honor, I know what's wrong with
        him. He can't help it.
        He was hypnotized last night.

CALLAHAN
Is that why he held up the liquor store?

DUANE
Benny, listen to me. Think of something sad like starving orphans.

(Benny sobers for an instant and then breaks up again)

MARIAN
Wilma, try to remember the key word to make him stop. The hypnotist must have said it.

WILMA
He was just about to say it, when the cop came running in.

DUANE
Let's just hope Marian can contact that hypnotist and Find out how to bring Benny out of this.

MARIAN LEAVES TO CALL THE HYPNOTIST.

WILMA
The Judge is going to be back any minute now to send us to jail.
    (Wilma starts to cry which makes Benny laugh more)

MARIAN COMES BACK IN.

DUANE
Did you get Miller on the phone?

MARIAN

No. I talked to his landlady and she said one
of the other tenants saw Miller leaving last
night with his luggage. She was very upset. It
seems Miller owed her two months of rent.

WILMA

Oh, Benny, you were right about him. He is
a crook.

MARIAN

What do we do now?

DUANE

Let me try. Benny, I'll give you twenty
bucks if you stop laughing.

(Benny makes a real effort to stop
laughing.)

BENNY

Do I hear thirty?

WILMA

That's it. I'll see you all in five or ten years.

DUANE

Oh, Wilma, you can't give up hope.

MARIAN

Benny's like a man possessed. You're going
to be a minister,
Duane, try saying a prayer over him.

BAILIFF

(yelling)
Time's up folks.

WILMA

Hurry and say that prayer, Duane.

DUANE WALKS OVER TO BENNY WHO IS STILL LAUGHING AND
EXTENDS HIS HAND OVER HIM.

DUANE

Dear Lord…

INSTANTLY BENNY STOPPED LAUGHING AND STANDS UP.
EVERYONE IS SURPRISED, ESPECIALLY DUANE.

MARIAN

Wow! It's a miracle.

BENNY

No it's not. That's what Miller said when
the cop ran in to the classroom.

DUANE

Oh…gee…

WILMA

It doesn't matter, Duane. I think you're
wonderful.

BENNY

You want to see wonderful. Watch me
dazzle this Judge.

THE JUDGE COMES BACK IN.

WILMA

It was right at this point that the real miracle
occurred. Benny didn't get a chance to say

another word. It seems while we were trying
to get Benny to stop laughing, the police
arrested
the guy that Benny borrowed the clothes
from, and he confessed to
robbing the liquor store. The charges
against us were dropped.

CALLAHAN

Case dismissed!

A WEEK LATER: WILMA, BENNY AND DUANE ARE TOGETHER.

WILMA

Benny would have hounded me to the grave
if I didn't keep my promise, so I convinced
Marian to go out with him. Anyway, the
party was a real dud, until Benny started
talking about the hypnotism class
and our day in court.
Everyone loved the story and the other girls
gave Benny a lot of attention and said how
funny and cute he was.
I guess that was what convinced Marian to
keep dating him. Or maybe she just felt
guilty for taking the fifty dollars and my best
gold earrings.

CURTAIN

Carol Costa Bio

Stage/Television/Radio Credits

Plays Published:

- The Last Decent Crooks, Comedy Mystery Big Dog/Norman Maine
- Phantom of the Soap Opera, Melodrama Big Dog/Norman Maine
- Deadline Dilemma, Mystery Big Dog/Norman Maine
- Scenes from House of Broken Dreams, The Best Scenes for Kids from 7 to 15 Applause Books
- Across the Road, Children's Play, Lilleanos Publishing

Play Productions:

- Death Insurance
    Royal Court Repertory NYC
- Big Al Goes Straight, Winner of the Robert J. Pickering Award for Excellence in Playwrighting
    Tibbets Opera House Coldwater, MI
    Royal Court Repertory NYC
    La Maison Theatre, Los Angeles
- The Last Decent Crooks aka Big Al Goes Straight
    Dance Theater Long Beach, CA
    Norwalk Players Norwalk, OH
    River Cities Community Theater, Bullhead City, AZ
- A Matter of Life of Death
    Quaigh Theatre NYC
    Hammond Community Theatre, Hammond, IN
    Room 5 Players, Tucson, AZ
- Deadline Dilemma
    Mill Mountain Theatre, Roanoke, VA
    American Theatre, San Diego, CA
- Phantom of the Soap Opera
    Written for my son's high school drama class and has now been produced more than twenty times in the Tucson high schools. The version published is a revised script.

Television Productions:
- My Bargain with God - segments featured on Sightings on Fox and Beyond Chance on Lifetime
- Psychic Evidence - segment featured on Sightings

Radio Productions:
- The Listing Appointment, Til Death Due Us Part, Deadline Dilemma - KCSN Los Angeles, CA "30 minutes to Curtain"

Carol was born and raised in Chicago. She now lives in Tucson where she donates her directing and comedy writing skills to fundraising show in local theaters. Carol is also the author of more than thirty books, including two best selling mystery series. With a business background in public accounting, Carol has written five financial titles for Penguin/Random House. For more information look up Carol Costa up on Amazon.com

Made in the
USA
Lexington, KY